The Ugly Duckling

Jackie Walter and Sarah Horne

W
FRANKLIN WATTS
LONDON • SYDNEY

1
The Biggest Egg

Once upon a time, Mother Duck sat waiting patiently for her eggs to hatch. Each egg was precious, and she hardly dared move in case any of the eggs got cold without her.

Before too long, she heard a tap-tap-tapping. Then she heard a crack-crack-cracking. And next there came a cheep-cheep-cheeping from four tiny, fluffy yellow ducklings who popped excitedly out of their shells.

But from the biggest egg, Mother Duck could hear nothing. She began to worry so she tapped lightly on the shell. "Are you all right in there?" she asked. Still she heard nothing. "It's time to come out now!" she called a little louder.

5

Finally, she heard a loud tap-tap-tapping and
a crack-crack-cracking. Out of the biggest egg
came a very large, very grey duckling.

Mother Duck was a bit surprised that this duckling looked so different, but she was very relieved he had hatched safely. "Come along then, dear. It's time for all of you to have your first swimming lesson. Follow me!"

2
The Swimming Lesson

Mother Duck proudly took her ducklings
to the pond. They dived in happily and
splashed about, and the large, ugly
duckling was the best swimmer of all.

8

But the other birds were mean. They couldn't stop laughing at how the duckling looked and they started to tease him.

9

The meanest bird came right up to him.
"You're the ugliest duckling I ever did see
and there's no place on this farm for you,"
he quacked. Mother Duck was furious.
"You leave him alone," she quacked back.
"He's my duckling and I love him. And he's
a far better swimmer than you will ever be!"

But the other birds joined in with the teasing and laughing, and the poor duckling was frightened. He ran as far away as his little legs would carry him. Mother Duck looked everywhere, but the little duckling was nowhere to be found.

3
Lost!

The ugly duckling soon got lost. On he wandered until he reached a marsh. Some geese started to laugh at him. "You look very odd!" they honked loudly. "What kind of bird are you?"

The ugly duckling hung his head sadly. "Everybody thinks I look strange," he whimpered. "I wish I could find some friends, but I don't think I'll find any here."

On and on the ugly duckling walked until
he could walk no further. He found a tiny
cottage and snuggled beneath a nearby
bush. He curled into a tight ball and fell fast
asleep as the sun set.

The ugly duckling
awoke to the sound of
noisy clucking. A bossy
hen stood over him.
"Who are you and
what can you do?"
she asked rudely.
"Erm, I'm good at swimming…"
the ugly duckling began.
"Can you lay eggs?" demanded the hen.
"I don't think so," said the duckling.
"Then this is no home for you!" squawked
the hen. "Only useful birds like me can stay
here. Be off with you, at once!"

The ugly duckling once again ran off as quickly as he could.

4
The Riverbank

Before too long, the ugly duckling came
to a riverbank. Nobody laughed at him or
told him to leave, so he decided to stay and
hide there. He did feel lonely, and he often
wished for some other birds to talk to.

One day, he saw three beautiful white birds soaring above the river. They looked so graceful and happy. "If only I were more like them," he sighed miserably, "then nobody would laugh at me or chase me away."

A few weeks later, autumn arrived.
The leaves on the trees turned red and
golden, and a chilly wind blew them in
swirls around the duckling's hiding place.
He felt even lonelier as the other animals
left the river to sleep or find a warmer home
for the winter.

Not long after that, winter came. Snow covered the riverbank like a blanket and the river iced over. The ugly duckling was hungry, cold and lonelier than he had ever felt before.

5
The Beautiful White Birds

As winter turned to spring, the ugly duckling made a decision. "I cannot stay here forever," he told himself firmly. "I must find my family or meet some friends. Otherwise I will die of loneliness."

With that, the ugly duckling swam up the river until he came to a pond. And there, gliding gracefully on the water and causing barely a ripple, were the same three beautiful white birds he had seen above the river.

"Here goes!" thought the ugly duckling
bravely. "Unless I try to talk to them, I will
never know whether they will be my friends
or not. All they can do is laugh or tell me to
go away. And if they do that, then I will just
find some other friends."

He took a really deep breath, looked down into the still water of the pond and gasped as he saw his reflection.

"Is that me? Can that really be me?" The ugly duckling's feathers were now glossy and white. His neck was long and graceful. He was really a beautiful white bird, just like the others!

The other swans had glided silently up
behind him. "Hello there, young swan!" they
called. "Why are you swimming all on your
own? Would you like to join us?"

And the beautiful swan, who never had been an ugly duckling after all, giggled happily. "Yes, please!" he laughed. "And then I need to find Mother Duck and tell her all about my adventures!"

About the story

The Ugly Duckling was written by Hans Christian Andersen and was included in his collection *New Fairy Tales* published in 1843. It is an original story and does not come from an existing fairy tale or folklore.

Hans Christian Andersen was born in Denmark in 1805. He wrote plays, travel books, novels and poems, but he is best remembered for his fairy tales, and *The Ugly Duckling* is the most famous of these. The story is popular around the world as a tale about change and transformation. The story has inspired a Walt Disney film as well as a Russian opera, popular songs, a musical and a television series.

Be in the story!

Imagine you are the ugly duckling when you are being chased away again. What would you like to say to the bossy hen?

Now imagine you are the ugly duckling when you have just looked down into the water and seen your reflection. What would you like to say to the animals who were mean to you?

Franklin Watts
First published in Great Britain in 2016 by The Watts Publishing Group

Text © Franklin Watts 2016
Illustrations © Sarah Horne 2009

The right of Sarah Horne to be identified as the illustrator
of this Work have been asserted in accordance with the
Copyright, Designs and Patents Act, 1988.

A CIP catalogue record for this book is available
from the British Library.

The artwork for this story first appeared in
Hopscotch Fairy Tales: The Ugly Duckling

ISBN 978 1 4451 4649 2 (hbk)
ISBN 978 1 4451 4651 5 (pbk)
ISBN 978 1 4451 4650 8 (library ebook)

Series Editor: Jackie Hamley
Series Advisor: Catherine Glavina
Series Designer: Cathryn Gilbert

Printed in China

Franklin Watts
An imprint of
Hachette Children's Group
Part of The Watts Publishing Group
Carmelite House
50 Victoria Embankment
London EC4Y 0DZ

An Hachette UK Company
www.hachette.co.uk

www.franklinwatts.co.uk

FSC
www.fsc.org
MIX
Paper from
responsible sources
FSC® C104740